W9-AZC-492

# Thomas and James

**The Rev. W. Awdry**
**Illustrated by Robin Davies**

Every morning The Fat Controller came to the station to catch
his train. He always said "Hello" to Thomas the Tank Engine.
Thomas worked hard every day pushing and pulling all the
trucks into the right places.
"I need to learn all about the trucks to become a Really Useful
Engine," Thomas told himself.

There were some funny-looking trucks in a siding. There was a small coach, some flat trucks, and a strange thing that his Driver called a crane.

"That's the breakdown train," said the Driver. "When there is an accident, the engine takes the workmen to clear and mend the line. The crane is for lifting heavy things, like engines, coaches and trucks."

One day, Thomas was in the Yard, when he heard an engine whistling "Help! Help!" A goods train came rushing through much too quickly.

The engine was a new engine called James and he was very frightened. His brake blocks were on fire, and flames and sparks were streaming out on each side.

"They're pushing me! They're pushing me!" panted James.

"On! On! On! On!" laughed the trucks, pushing James along the rails. "Help! Help!" whistled James as he disappeared out of sight.

"I hope James will be alright," thought Thomas, but it was already too late. The trucks pushed James right off the rails!

Suddenly a bell rang in the signal box and a man came running down the Yard towards Thomas.

"James is off the line – we must get the breakdown train – quickly!" shouted the man.

Thomas was coupled on, the workmen jumped into the coach and off they went as fast as they could.

"Hurry! Hurry! Hurry!" puffed Thomas, working as hard as he could.

They found James and the trucks on a bend in the line.
The brake van and the last few trucks were still on the rails,
but the front ones were piled in a heap next to James.

Poor James was looking very unhappy.
"I'd like to teach those trucks a lesson," thought Thomas.

James' Driver and Fireman were feeling him
all over to see if he was hurt.
"Never mind, James," said the Fireman.
"It wasn't your fault," said the Driver. "It was those
wooden brakes. We always said they were no good."

**Thomas used the breakdown train to pull the unhurt trucks
out of the way. He worked hard all afternoon, pulling all the
other trucks back to the Yard as well.**

"This'll teach you a lesson! This'll teach you a lesson!"
Thomas told the trucks.
"Yes it will, yes it will," they said in sad, creaky voices.

The workmen mended the line and then lifted James back onto the rails with the crane.
"Steady!" said one of the workmen, as they lifted James into the air.
"Carefully now," said another, as they put James back onto the rails.
"Oh dear, I can't move!" said James.

Thomas took James back to the engine shed to be mended.
The Fat Controller was waiting for them, anxiously.
"I'm very pleased with you, Thomas," said The Fat Controller.

"You're a Really Useful Engine. We'll give James some new
brakes and a shiny new coat of paint, and Thomas – you shall
have a branch line all to yourself."
"Oh, thank you, Sir!" said Thomas, happily.

Thomas was very happy to have his very own branch line. He puffed proudly backwards and forwards with two coaches every day.

Best of all, Thomas liked picking up all the passengers at the stations and taking them on their journey.

Thomas often saw the other engines at the junctions.
Some of them stopped to say hello, and some, like Gordon,
didn't have time to stop, but said "Poop, poop!" as they
rushed past.
And Thomas always whistled "Peep, peep!" in return.